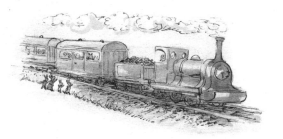

The Railway Rabbits

Wisher and the
Runaway Piglet

Collect all the Railway Rabbits books now!

The Railway Rabbits

Wisher and the
Runaway Piglet

Georgie Adams

Illustrated by Anna Currey

Orion
Children's Books

First published in Great Britain in 2010
This new edition published in 2014
by Orion Children's Books
a division of the Orion Publishing Group Ltd
Orion House
5 Upper St Martin's Lane
London WC2H 9EA

An Hachette UK company

1 3 5 7 9 10 8 6 4 2

A catalogue record for this book is available from the British Library.

ISBN 978 1 4440 1197 5

Printed in Great Britain by Clays Ltd, St Ives plc

www.orionbooks.co.uk

For Mia Barclay Errington –
with love G.A.

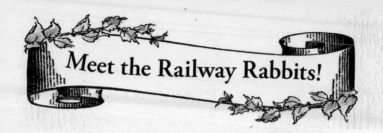

Meet the Railway Rabbits!

Wisher Longears

The smallest of the
Longears children,
Wisher has silvery-white
fur and pink ears.
She wears a kerchief
around her neck.

Personality: Quiet and thoughtful, but
with an adventurous side. When something
unusual is about to happen, her ears tingle!

Likes: Exploring, mysteries, her best friend,
Parsley Mole.

Dislikes: People-folk, being the centre of
attention because of her special powers.

Favourite saying: "My ears are tingling!"

Bramble Longears

Bramble is the biggest and bossiest of the rabbits. He has a shiny, jet-black coat, and wears a stripy scarf.

Personality: A fearless and adventurous rabbit, Bramble loves to be the leader and is very competitive.

Likes: Winning races, playing with his friends Tansy and Teasel.

Dislikes: Losing to his brother Bracken, not being the leader.

Favourite saying: "Wriggly worms!"

Bracken Longears

Bracken has pale, gingery-brown fur and ears with black tips. He wears a spotty kerchief around his neck.

Personality: Like Bramble, he loves adventure, but isn't quite as brave as his brother. He's the fastest, though, and always wins races!

Likes: Running fast, working out problems without Bramble's help, his friend Nigel.

Dislikes: Not being in charge.

Favourite saying: "Slugs and snails!"

Berry Longears

Berry has a reddish-
brown coat with white
tail, tummy and paws.
He wears a jacket.

Personality: Berry can always be relied
on to cheer everyone up with a joke. He is
always falling over and getting himself into
trouble.

Likes: Corncobs, jokes and Fern, his
favourite sister.

Dislikes: Monsters, especially the beasts that
hide in the maze at Fairweather's Farm Park.

Favourite saying: "Creeping caterpillars!"

Fern Longears

Fern has a soft grey coat with fern-like black markings between her ears, a white tummy and two front paws. She wears a daisy chain around her neck.

Personality: Fern is a worrier and often assumes the worst will happen, but she is also inquisitive, creative and good at finding things.

Likes: Stories, singing, hunting for pretty shiny objects.

Dislikes: Owls, rats and any kind of danger to herself and her brothers and sisters.

Favourite saying: "Bugs and beetles!"

Mellow Longears

Mellow has grey-brown fur, a white nose and big, soft eyes. She wears a straw hat decorated with flowers.

Personality: Sensible and well-organised. She loves all her children, but pays special attention to Wisher, who needs extra protection because of her gift.

Likes: Flowers, chatting to her friends Daisy Duck and Sylvia Squirrel.

Dislikes: Silliness, untidiness and the Red Dragon.

Favourite saying: "Silly rabbits have careless habits."

Barley Longears

Barley has black and white fur, and unusually long ears. He wears a waistcoat with barley straws in his pocket.

Personality: A real worrier! Barley cares about his family, and spends most of his time keeping a sharp watch for trouble.

Likes: His favourite look-out tree stump, his best friend Blinker Badger.

Dislikes: Burdock the Buzzard.

Favourite saying: "Oh, buttercups!"

THE LONGEARS / SILVERCOAT FAMILIES

BARLEYCORN LONGEARS
of DEEP BURROW
GREAT - GREAT - ELDER PARR

BUTTERWORT LONGEARS
& POPPY
GREAT - ELDER PARR
& GREAT - ELDER MARR
LONGEARS

BLACKBERRY LONGEARS
& PRIMROSE
ELDER PARR & ELDER MARR
LONGEARS

MEADOW SILVERCOAT
of CASTLE HILL
AND GREAT - GREAT - ELDER MARR

WOODRUFF SILVERCOAT
& MALLOW
GREAT - ELDER PARR
& GREAT - ELDER MARR
SILVERCOAT

EYEBRIGHT SILVERCOAT
& WILLOW
ELDER PARR & ELDER MARR
SILVERCOAT

BARLEY LONGEARS AND MELLOW SILVERCOAT
PARR AND MARR

BRAMBLE   BRACKEN   BERRY   FERN   WISHER
BUCK   BUCK   BUCK   DOE   DOE

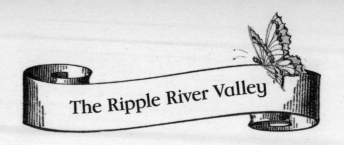

The Ripple River Valley

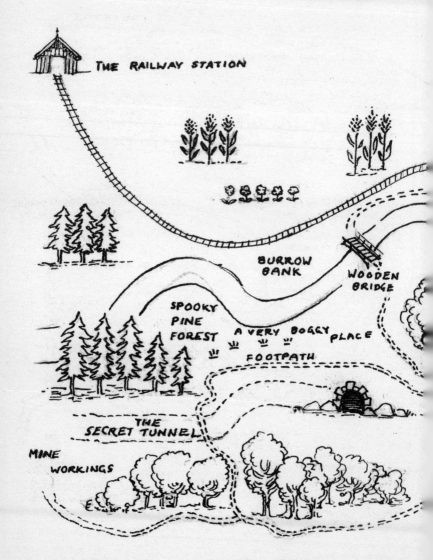

THE RAILWAY STATION

BURROW BANK

WOODEN BRIDGE

SPOOKY PINE FOREST

A VERY BOGGY PLACE

FOOTPATH

THE SECRET TUNNEL

MINE WORKINGS

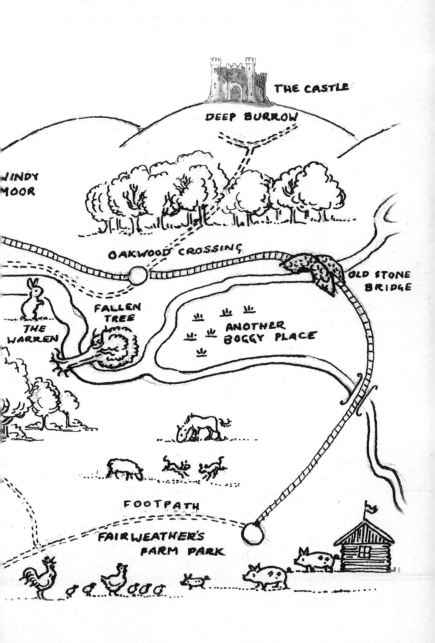

The New Arrivals

1

Mellow Longears was expecting her first babies, and today was the day. Her husband, Barley Longears, was hopping around the burrow making sure Mellow had everything she needed.

"Here's another pillow," said Barley, placing a soft, mossy cushion behind her back. He had already brought her three plump pillows, so there wasn't much room for any more. "Are you warm enough?" he asked anxiously. "Perhaps you're too hot?

Your ears look pinker than usual.
Shall I bring you some tea? Yes, a sip of
tea might be just the thing. Would you
like dandelion . . . cowslip . . . or both?
Oh dear, I can't decide! Maybe sorrel
tea would be better . . ."

"Barley Longears!" said Mellow. "Do
stop fussing. Just leave me to get on with
things. I'll call you when I'm ready."

Barley could tell from Mellow's tone
that she meant what she said. He kissed

her on the nose and went outside.

Barley made straight for his favourite look-out place, a tree stump near the warren. From here he could see the River Ripple. He had unusually long ears for a rabbit and his hearing was excellent. It was how he had got his name. For a while he sat and listened to the soothing sounds of the river as it swished along, tumbling over rocks. He knew this In-Not-Such-A-Hurry River so well. It lazily wound its way between steeply wooded hills and a patchwork of fields. Barley Longears had lived in this part of the river valley for as long as he could remember, and he wouldn't dream of living anywhere else.

From his tree stump, Barley could also see the tracks of the Red Dragon. He knew all about the monster that roared along the valley every day – up and down, up and down – whistling loudly and belching clouds of smoke. Although it looked a terrifying beast Barley had never once seen it stray from its tracks. He knew where it was likely to be and how to avoid it, unlike his number one enemy, Burdock the buzzard, who could suddenly swoop from the sky to attack. Barley's tree stump was a good place to keep watch for Burdock. He looked up at a telegraph pole, where the huge bird often perched, waiting to catch a rabbit. But today, much to Barley's relief, Burdock was nowhere in sight.

It was springtime and already Barley had noticed the days growing longer. The smell of sweet new grass filled the air. Now, as he watched the late afternoon sun slip behind some fir trees, he sighed and said:

"Spring. The *perfect* time to start a family!"

Suddenly he heard a rustling in the reeds nearby and heard a voice say:

"Family? Did you say . . . *family?*"

Barley looked round to see his friend, Violet Vole, peering at him.

"Hello, Violet," said Barley. "Yes, babies. Any minute. Any *second*. Oh, buttercups! Just think. Our warren will soon be full of baby rabbits."

Violet chuckled.

"Well," she said, "I didn't think it would be full of baby *hedgehogs!*

Congratulations, Barley Longears. Can't stop. Must hurry back to my nest. I have babies of my own to feed. We're having slugs for supper. Goodbye."

Barley watched Violet slip down the bank into the river. He was just wondering if he should see how Mellow was getting on when his good friend, Blinker Badger, appeared.

"Nice evening to be out and about," said Blinker. "Care for a walk in the woods?"

"Sorry, Blinker," said Barley.
"I'm waiting for my babies to arrive.
I'm about to become *Parr* Longears."

"Splendid news!" said Blinker. "And a
very fine parr you'll be, Barley Longears.
Have cubs of my own. It's hard work
bringing up a family. Fun too, of course.
Nothing like a game of rough and tumble
with the cubs!"

"I've obviously got a lot to learn,"
said Barley.

"You'll learn as you go along," said
Blinker. "All parents do! Now, I must find
some worms for supper. Goodbye."

Barley watched Blinker trundling
across the meadow, until a movement
in the branches of an oak caught his
attention. He saw a flash of white fur,
then an animal with a grey, bushy tail
came scurrying towards him. It was
Sylvia Squirrel.

"I couldn't help overhearing what you were saying to Violet and Blinker," said Sylvia. "Babies! How exciting. Lots of mouths to feed and children can be such a worry, can't they? I'm told you have to watch them *all* the time. Can't let them out of your sight for a second. One blink and they're off and up to all sorts. *Such* a worry. But a joy, I'm sure. Sadly I don't have any children but I hear they can be quite exhausting!"

"Oh," said Barley. "I hadn't thought. Yes, I suppose you're right. Lots to think about as you say and . . ."

"Sorry. Can't stop," said Sylvia. "I buried some hazelnuts around here somewhere. I must find them before dark or I won't have any supper. Good luck with your babies. Goodbye!"

Sylvia hurried away, leaving Barley pacing up and down, tugging first one ear, then the other.

"As if waiting for babies to arrive isn't worrying enough," said Barley. "It seems I'll have even *more* to worry about after they're born!"

Just then he heard Mellow softly calling to him from the burrow, and he raced inside.

"Five," said Mellow proudly. "We have five beautiful babies, *Parr* Longears!"

Barley liked the way Mellow said Parr Longears. His eyes twinkled as he said:

"Are you sure, *Marr* Longears?" He blinked in wonder at the five small bundles cradled in Mellow's arms.

"Quite sure," she replied. "I've counted them *twice*. Three boys and two girls."

Barley was so excited he flipped a backward somersault, then ran round the burrow singing:

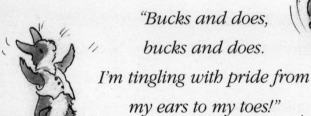

"Bucks and does,
bucks and does.
I'm tingling with pride from
my ears to my toes!"

Later that evening when the tiny rabbits were asleep in their beds, Mellow whispered:

"We must name our babies before sunrise, Barley."

"Of course," he said. "It's unlucky for newborns to pass one whole night without a name. It would never do!"

The two proud parents spent a while thinking of names for their children, during which time there was much scratching of ears and twitching of whiskers. At last, as the moon disappeared behind a hill, they had made up their minds.

Well, almost. Mellow was not quite sure about one name.

"Bramble Longears, Bracken Longears and Berry Longears for the bucks," said Barley.

"Fern Longears and . . ." Mellow hesitated, pausing to look again at her last-born who had silvery-white fur and

was so much smaller than the others. She
didn't know why, but she had a feeling
there was something unusual – something
special – about this little doe.

"Well?" said Barley. "Fern and . . .
what?"

"Wisher," said Mellow. "We shall call
her Wisher Longears!"

Then the sun rose in the dawn sky to
welcome them all.

First Day Out

2

Mellow's nest for her babies was tucked
away at one end of a burrow. She knew
it was the safest place for her young to
grow in their first few weeks of life. She
had lined a bed with soft fur, groomed
from her own coat. It was what all good
mother rabbits did to keep their little ones
warm. Their cosy home smelled sweetly
of earth and tree roots, but there wasn't
much room to move around. After filling
their tummies with Mellow's milk, the five

young rabbits were content to snuggle up together and fall asleep.

During this time, Mellow and Barley did everything they could to protect the little rabbits in their home underground. They knew only too well that a cunning fox might smell the babies and try to dig them out of the burrow. Barley spent many long hours on guard duty outside the warren, while Mellow kept watch below.

And so the days went by, until . . . three whole weeks had passed since the birth of the five baby rabbits. Bramble, Bracken, Berry, Fern and Wisher had been growing fast and were ready to come out of the warren. Today was their very first outing!

Before they set off, Barley gathered the children inside the burrow to give them some good advice. He was anxious that nothing should go wrong on this special day.

"We must all stay together," he said. "The world *up-burrow* is a wonderful place. Sunshine, fresh air and plenty to eat! But there are dangers. You must keep your wits about you at all times. Burdock the buzzard would love to have one of you for breakfast. Or a hungry fox. And beware of the Red Dragon!"

The five young rabbits looked at one another. They remembered the stories Parr had told them about those scary creatures.

"Oh, Parr! I don't want to be eaten by Burdock," said Fern. She huddled close to Berry for comfort.

"I don't want to be eaten by ANYTHING!" said Berry brightly. "Don't worry, Fern. I'll look after you."

"Huh! I'm not scared," said Bramble boldly. He was the biggest of the five young rabbits and already he seemed quite fearless. Once or twice Mellow had caught him venturing along one of the tunnels, eager to explore.

"If I met a fox," said Bramble. "I'd box him on the nose!"

Bracken looked at his big brother. His tummy flipped at the very thought of seeing a fox, but he wanted to show he was as brave as Bramble.

"Yes, you punch his nose and I'll pull his tail!" he said.

Wisher, meanwhile, had been half-listening to this chatter and half-daydreaming.

"I wonder what the Red Dragon looks like?" she said. She'd tried to picture the monster Parr had described so many times, racing up and down the valley, breathing fire and smoke. She felt curious and afraid at the same time. Perhaps I'll see him today, she thought.

Mellow looked at Wisher. What *was* her daughter thinking? she wondered.

"Always listen to your parr," said Mellow. "You'll be all right if you're sensible and stay close. Remember, only silly rabbits have careless habits!"

"I'll be on the look-out for trouble," Barley said.

"If I need to warn you of danger, or want you to come to me, I'll send a signal. Like this."

He thumped his hind foot on the burrow floor three times – *thump, thump, thump!*

Wisher felt the sounds vibrating round the walls. Barley told them they would feel the sounds above ground too, then he said:

"Time to go. Follow me!"

He took everyone along a newly made tunnel, over tree roots and up

a slope, until at last they arrived at an entrance to their warren.

Barley went outside, sniffed the air and looked about cautiously. When he was sure it was safe, he called:

"All clear!"

Mellow led the way, bringing her five young rabbits from the familiar dimness of their home out into the bright world above. She watched with pride as, one by one, the rabbits hopped out.

Bramble leapt
away from the burrow.
Mellow admired his
glossy black coat and
ears. "Hurry up," he shouted to the others.
"You're as slow as snails!"

Bracken was close
behind. Mellow thought
he was well named with
his pale, gingery fur which
looked just like bracken in the
autumn. His ears were black-tipped.

"Coming!" he cried "Wait for me."

Next came Berry. He
gave his marr a cheeky grin
and flipped a somersault! His
reddish-brown fur looked red
as a rosehip in the sunshine.

"Here I come!" shouted Berry.

Fern crept after her brothers. Mellow thought she looked beautiful with her soft, grey coat and wispy, fern-like hair between her ears. "I'm hungry," said Fern, chasing after Berry.

Mellow waited for her last-born. Wisher's small, silvery-white head and two pink ears appeared at the entrance. Then she hopped outside.

"Sorry," said Wisher. "I must have been daydreaming."

Mellow smiled. Yes, she thought. Wisher is not like her brothers and sisters. She's different.

"Come along," she said gently. "Let's catch up with the others. We must look for something to eat."

The early morning sun was warm on their
backs as Barley and Mellow set about
teaching the five young Longears where
to look for food. They nibbled grass
and juicy dandelion leaves, their noses
twitching with excitement at all the new
scents of the up-burrow.

After a while, Wisher found herself
alone. She sat among some primroses,
gazing around this strange new world.
She thought it looked so big compared to
her little nest in the warren.

Not far off she could see Parr sitting
on his tree stump, watching the skies for
Burdock. Near a bush Marr was busily
washing and grooming her soft, grey-
brown fur. Bramble, Bracken, Berry
and Fern had stopped eating and were
playing a game of Hop-Back.

When they'd tired of this, Wisher saw
Bramble point to a small wooden bridge
by the river and heard him say:

"Race you over there!"

"Where's Wisher?" said Berry, suddenly
aware that she was missing.

Fern spotted her sister.

"Hey, Wisher!" she cried. "We're having
a race."

"Coming!" said Wisher.

Mellow looked to see them all lining up at the start.

"Stay where I can see you," she warned.

"We will," said Bracken. "Ready, steady, GO!"

They raced towards the little bridge. Bracken got there first, and Bramble was second. The others ran up panting and out of breath.

"Phew!" said Fern to Bracken. "You were *so* fast."

"I could have won if I'd wanted to," said Bramble. "I'm going to explore the other side of the bridge. I might find something interesting . . ."

"Yes. Something like Burdock the buzzard!" said Berry. "That *would* be interesting."

"Please, don't go, Bramble," said Fern nervously. "Burdock could be *anywhere*."

"Well, I'm going anyway," said Bramble. "You can stay behind if you want to."

"I'll come," said Bracken. He knew he'd upset Bramble by winning the race and now saw his chance to please him.

"Okay," said Fern, who didn't want the bucks to think she was scared. "Coming, Wisher?"

Everyone looked at Wisher. She had a faraway look in her eyes and seemed puzzled about something.

"I don't know . . ." she said slowly. "My ears are tingling. I think I can hear a voice inside my head."

"Spooky," said Berry.

"What does it say?" asked Fern.

Wisher told them:

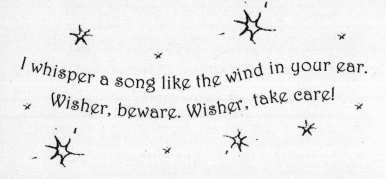

I whisper a song like the wind in your ear.
Wisher, beware. Wisher, take care!

Wisher didn't understand how or why
she seemed to be the only one able to hear
this voice. All she knew was that it was a
sign there might be danger ahead.

Bramble rolled his eyes.

"You're just trying to scare us," he said.
"I'm off!"

But Wisher's words had made everyone
else feel uneasy.

"I-I think we should go after Bramble," said Bracken. "He might want our help."

The others agreed, so they followed Bramble across the bridge and caught up with him. He was sitting at the bottom of a steep railway embankment. Although Bramble didn't say so, he was very pleased to see them. After Wisher's mysterious warning, even *he* didn't want to explore on his own.

"Let's see what's up there," he said.

The five young rabbits scampered to the top and came at once to the railway line.

"Ooo!" said Fern, looking up and down the line. "Remember Parr telling us about the Red Dragon? These must be his tracks!"

"Told you," said Bramble. "I said I'd find something interesting."

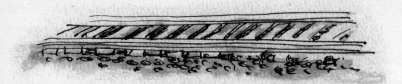

As Wisher stared at the tracks, words
from the strange song came back to her:

*I whisper a song like the wind in your ear.
Wisher, beware. Wisher, take care!*

Despite the warning, she felt excited.

"What if the Red Dragon comes?"
she said.

"We run for our lives!" said Berry.

"Listen," said Bracken. "What was
that?"

The five young rabbits froze, expecting
to see the scary dragon. They listened.

A soft thudding noise came again –
thump, thump, thump! And they all felt
the ground shake . . .

Barley had seen them cross the bridge
and chased after them. He sat at the
bottom of the embankment, thumping his
foot on the ground.

*Thump, thump,
thump!*

Mellow came
rushing towards
them.

"You naughty
rabbits!" she
said. "It's very
dangerous here."

"Yes," said Barley, hopping up beside
her. "Didn't I warn you about the Red
Dragon? The monster comes along here
every day."

"He's always in a temper," said Mellow. "Spitting sparks and puffing smoke. You stay away from those tracks, young rabbits. Now, come along home. That's quite enough exploring for your first day out!"

The Dragon's Lair

3

One morning, a few days after her first
outing, Wisher was wandering along
by herself and daydreaming. She'd
left Bramble, Bracken, Berry and Fern
playing Tag-and-Tumble, after the game
had got too rough. Marr had shooed them
all out of the warren, so she could get on
with some spring cleaning. Parr was at
his usual tree stump, deep in conversation
with Blinker the badger, so he didn't
notice Wisher go off on her own.

There
was plenty
for Wisher to think
about as she hopped along that morning.
In the short while she'd been exploring
up-burrow she'd discovered many new
things: the tastiest plants to eat; the
best kind of tree bark to gnaw; and the
prettiest wildflowers to sniff – she thought
the smell of primroses was probably her
favourite.

But there had been scary moments
too. Once she'd seen the shadow of a big
bird in the sky, hovering near her warren.

She'd been sure it was Burdock. She had frozen to the spot for a moment, unable to move a muscle, before dashing home – her heart pounding.

And then there was the Red Dragon! Wisher had been with Fern and Berry when they'd first seen it a long way off, clattering along its tracks and puffing clouds of smoke. Wisher thought she'd seen flames too, as the monster roared along the valley. Even from a distance, it looked a terrifying sight.

Near a small heap of freshly dug earth, Wisher stopped to pick a dandelion clock. She blew its fluffy seeds and watched them fly away. It's *such* an exciting world up here! she thought dreamily. And I've so much more to discover . . .

Just then she felt the ground beneath her feet tremble. A few seconds later, she heard someone behind her say:

"Excuse me. You're in my way."

Wisher spun round. Peering up at her was an animal with a silky black coat and pointed nose.

"Er, hello," said Wisher, a little nervously. "Who are you?"

"Mole," said the animal. "My friends call me Parsley. Come to think of it, I haven't got many friends. Too busy tunnelling, you see."

"My name's Wisher," said Wisher. She'd never met a mole before, but there was something about Parsley she liked. Perhaps it was his friendly voice, or the way he squinted at her with his tiny eyes, or waved his big front paws about. Whatever it was, Wisher had a good feeling about Parsley.

After they'd talked for a while, Wisher discovered that Parsley knew his way below ground very well.

"Tunnels," said Parsley. "A great way to get about. Safer too. I can get from here to there and back again by tunnel. Backwards. Forwards. No fuss. No bother."

"I know about burrows," said Wisher brightly.

"Excellent," said Parsley. "We burrowers should stick together. Up the Burrowers, I say!"

Wisher laughed.

"I'd like to be your friend," she said.

"Then friends we shall be!" said
Parsley.

A moment later, they heard a piercing
whistle in the distance.

"Oh no," said Parsley. 'That's the Red
Dragon. When I hear him whistle, I know
he's awake. Makes my tunnels shake as
he goes by."

"I saw him once," said Wisher. "He
looked *very* angry."

"Hm! All huff, puff and smoke that
one," said Parsley.

"Do you know where he lives?"
asked Wisher.

Despite her parents' warnings, she
couldn't help wanting to know more
about the Red Dragon.

"Yes," said Parsley. "I'll show you
one day."

"Can we go today?" asked Wisher.
"Please."

"Well . . ." began Parsley. "I've just
started digging a new tunnel. But I
suppose it can wait. Come with me, my
friend. We're off to the Dragon's lair!"

Parsley said it was quicker to travel
underground, so Wisher followed her new
friend down a hole.

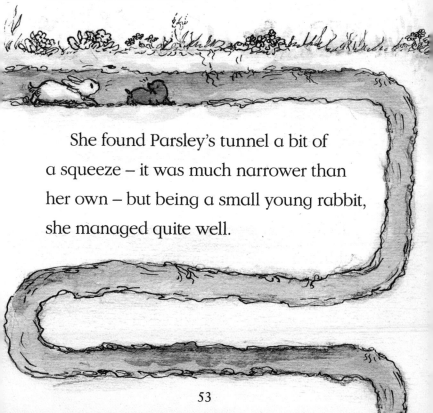

She found Parsley's tunnel a bit of
a squeeze – it was much narrower than
her own – but being a small young rabbit,
she managed quite well.

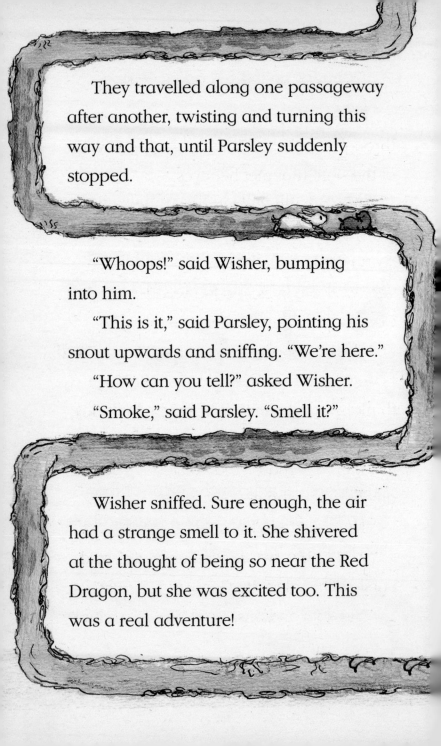

They travelled along one passageway after another, twisting and turning this way and that, until Parsley suddenly stopped.

"Whoops!" said Wisher, bumping into him.

"This is it," said Parsley, pointing his snout upwards and sniffing. "We're here."

"How can you tell?" asked Wisher.

"Smoke," said Parsley. "Smell it?"

Wisher sniffed. Sure enough, the air had a strange smell to it. She shivered at the thought of being so near the Red Dragon, but she was excited too. This was a real adventure!

"Up we go," said Parsley.

The two friends ran up a slope and out through a hole. Wisher's eyes opened wide at the sight that met her eyes.

"Where's the Red Dragon?" she whispered.

"Over there," said Parsley. "I can't see very well. He lives in a big wooden shed. Can you see him, Wisher? Is he there?"

"There's lots of smoke," said Wisher. "And I can hear a hissing noise. Ooooo! Yes, I think he's in there! Will he come out today, Parsley?"

"It all depends," said Parsley. "Are there any humans about?"

"Humans?" said Wisher.

"You know, two-legged animals," said Parsley. "People-folk. Can you see any?"

"Yes, lots and lots," said Wisher excitedly.

"Big ones. Small ones. There's a big one carrying a small one and . . ."

"Ah," said Parsley. "That means the Red Dragon *will* be coming out today. He takes people-folk for rides, you see."

"Wow!" exclaimed Wisher. "They must be very brave."

"Yes," said Parsley. "But they seem to enjoy themselves."

"Shall we stay till he comes out?" asked Wisher.

"Another day," said Parsley. "I've got a tunnel to dig. Remember?"

Wisher was disappointed, but she didn't want to argue with her new friend. She'd asked Parsley to show her where the Red Dragon lived, and he had. Besides, Wisher knew she should get home. If her parents discovered she was missing, she'd be in trouble!

The two hurried along the maze of passages and, in no time, arrived back where they'd started.

"Thank you," said Wisher. "Can we meet again soon?"

"Yes," said Parsley. "We will!"

Before Wisher could blink, he was gone. She felt the ground move slightly beneath her paws and knew it was Parsley – her friend had started tunnelling again.

Then Wisher raced home. She found Parr and Marr waiting for her by the warren.

"Where have you been?" said Barley crossly.

"We've been worrying our whiskers off about you!" said Mellow. And she gave Wisher a hug.

"I met a new friend," said Wisher. She told them all about Parsley and seeing the Red Dragon's lair.

Listening to Wisher tell of her adventures, Barley remembered what his friend, Sylvia Squirrel, had said on the day Wisher was born. "Children can be such a worry, can't they? I'm told you have to watch them *all* the time."

"I can see I'm going to have to keep my eye on you," said Barley.

Later, as she snuggled into her bed, Wisher's head was buzzing with all the exciting things she'd seen and done that day. Best of all, she thought, I've met Parsley. I hope I see him again soon.

And as she fell asleep that night, *something* told Wisher it wouldn't be long before she came face to face with the Red Dragon!

Trouble at Fairweathers
4

The Ripple Valley Steam Railway runs
from The Station, at one end of the line, to
Fred Fairweather's Farm Park at the other.
All the animals who lived at the Farm
Park knew that. They were used to seeing
visitors arrive by steam train, or by car,
every day.

One nosey ewe called Mrs Woolly
made it her business to know everything
that went on around the farm. Nothing
much escaped Mrs Woolly's eyes! And

because she liked to gossip, useful titbits
of information were quickly passed on to
her neighbours, and sometimes to other
animals living beyond the farm gates.

One morning, Mrs Woolly was
watching Fred Fairweather on his rounds.
As usual, the farmer fed Mrs Woolly
first – which she thought only right and
proper. She was happily munching hay
and keeping her eye on things, when
she spotted some visitors in the car park.
But Mrs Woolly was paying particular
attention to their dog. It was running
about and barking.

"Bah!" she huffed to a gaggle of geese who were her neighbours. "D'you see what I see? Dog! Off the lead, if I'm not mistaken. That means one thing. Trouble. You mark my words."

On hearing this alarming piece of news, the geese waddled about cackling:

"Dog on the loose! Oh, my feathers! What to do-do-do!"

The geese made such a racket that they attracted the dog's attention. He came bounding over to see what the fuss was about.

"Hello!" he said, wagging his tail. "I'm Toby. Can I come in?"

"No you can-not-not not!" cackled the frantic geese. "Oh, we shall all die-die-die! What a terrible to-do-do-doooooo!"

Mrs Woolly glared at Toby.

"There! See what you've done. Upset my neighbours, that's what. *They* won't be laying any eggs this morning. Bah! Dogs. Nothing but trouble in my opinion. Clear off!"

"Clear off yourself, *wool* head!" said Toby. Then he heard his mistress calling:

"Toby! *Tobeee!* Come here."

"Uh-oh," said Toby. "Better go before she catches me." He dashed off across the farmyard towards the pigs . . .

Agatha Old Spot, proud mother of seven beautiful piglets, watched Fred Fairweather slowly making his way round the farmyard. Agatha knew Fred kept to the same routine every morning at feeding time. First, he fed Mrs Woolly, and then the geese, chickens, goats and two Shetland ponies. Very soon it would be their turn.

"I'm hungry!" wailed one piglet called Foster. "My tummy's rumbling." As usual, Foster was impatient for his breakfast.

"Not long now," said Agatha. To take his mind off food, she added: "What a fine piglet you are, Foster. You're a perfect example of your breed, even though I say so myself."

Foster's tummy rumbled again.

"What's a breed?" he asked.

"In our case," replied Agatha, "a breed is a type of pig. We're Gloucester Old Spots."

Foster looked at his reflection in the shiny empty feeding bowl.

"Is that why I've got spots?" he said.

"Precisely," said Agatha. "Not *all* pigs have them. We are rather special. I named you after the farmer in a swine rhyme."

"Which one?" asked Foster.

"I'll tell you," said Agatha.

The other piglets gathered round to listen.

"Farmer Foster went to Gloucester,
Riding on a train.
He bought some pigs,
For a bag of figs,
And they all came home in the rain!"

Just then, Fred opened the pigsty door.
He was carrying a bucketful of warm,
milky slops and Foster thought it smelled
delicious! Foster ran up to Fred and
nuzzled his boot, trying to make sure he
was first to the bowl. The farmer tickled
Foster behind one ear, and began to pour
swill into the feeding bowl, as the other
piglets oinked in delight.

Unfortunately, at that moment, Toby the dog came bounding through the open door.

"Pigs! Pigs! Pigs!" he barked excitedly.

"Shoo!" shouted Fred.

But it was too late.

"Eeeeeek!" squealed seven panicking piglets, scattering in all directions and knocking over their food bucket.

"Oh, my poor piglets!" cried Agatha. She rushed at Toby, head down, snorting angrily. Agatha Old Spot was an enormous pig, and the sight of her charging like a bull was scary.

"I'm off!" cried Toby. He tore out of the pigsty, tail tucked between his legs. Then he spotted Foster. The little piglet had escaped from the sty and was running away as fast as he could.

Toby heard his mistress calling him again and again. She was getting closer

and Toby knew she would soon catch up
with him. Just time for *one* more game,
thought Toby. And he pelted after the
piglet . . .

Foster RAN as quickly as his little
legs could carry him. He flew across the
farmyard, up the railway embankment
and on to the line. When he'd last dared
look behind, that horrid dog was gaining
on him. Foster's heart was beating so
fast, he thought it would burst, but he
kept on running.

He had no
idea where he
was going. Foster
hurried down the middle
of the railway track. Every now and then
his trotters slipped on loose stones that
were packed between the rails. When
at last he came to a stone bridge, he
stopped to catch his breath.

"Oh," panted Foster. "I've never run so far in my life! I wonder where that terrible dog is?"

He turned first one way and then the other. Then to be quite sure he turned round the other way. The dog was nowhere in sight. It might be safe to go home now, he thought. But which way *was* home? He looked both ways down the track, but everything looked the same – railway lines and stones as far as he could see.

Foster sat down on top of the bridge. He was hungry, miserable and alone in a strange place. And he felt very, very afraid. Tears trickled down his cheeks. "I want to go home!" he cried.

Wisher Alone

5

News of the escaped piglet spread along the riverbank like wildfire. It began with Mrs Woolly and the geese, then one goose called Gilbert told the story to Daisy Duck who lived down by the river.

"Oh, it was terrible-terrible-terrible," gabbled Gilbert. "A monstrous dog! Or were there two? Poor Foster! Last seen running for his life. Don't know where he's gone-gone-gone."

"How dreadful!" quacked Daisy, and she paddled away down river. The first friend she met was Violet Vole.

"Have you heard?" said Daisy. "Foster the piglet is on the run. He's being chased by dogs. Two or three at least!"

"A terrible tale!" said Violet. "I must make sure my babies are safe." On the way to her nest in the riverbank, Violet met Sylvia Squirrel.

"Have you
heard?" said Violet.
"There's a piglet
running from a
pack of dogs.
Three or four
of them."

Sylvia
didn't wait to
hear any more. She dashed off to spread
the news as fast as she could.

"Have you heard?" she asked Blinker
Badger. "There's a pack of wild dogs on
the loose! They're chasing a piglet. Five
or six hungry dogs or more!"

"That's very bad news indeed!" said Blinker gravely. "I must go and warn my cubs."

On the way to his sett, Blinker met the Longears family. They were feeding near their warren.

"Have you heard?" said Blinker to Barley. "Wild dogs on the loose. Chasing a piglet. Six dogs at the very least!"

"Oh, buttercups!" exclaimed Barley. "As if we haven't enough to worry about. Burdock the buzzard, the Red Dragon and now a pack of wild dogs."

Mellow and the children stopped nibbling grass to listen. None of the young rabbits had seen a dog before – or a piglet for that matter.

Wild dogs! thought Wisher. They sound scary. And then she thought, poor piglet! I wonder what sort of animal it is?

"What do dogs look like?" asked Bramble.

"Well . . ." began Mellow slowly. "They come in all shapes and sizes. Some look like foxes, and are just as dangerous. Some don't. Their coats can be long, short, curly or straight and their tails . . ."

"Yes, yes," said Barley, interrupting. He could see the confused looks on his children's faces. "But the important thing is you must all be *extra* careful." He looked hard at Wisher. "And no running off on your own!"

Later that same morning, Wisher found herself alone again, just as she had been on her first day out of the burrow.

Parr had set himself extra guard duties, and had taken up his position on the tree stump. Marr was picking daisies to decorate her hat, and Bramble, Bracken, Berry and Fern were dozing in the sun.

"I'm going to look for Parsley," said Wisher to herself. "If he's tunnelling he might not have heard about the wild dogs." She'd been told not to wander off, but she had to warn her new friend, even if it meant getting into trouble.

Between the warren and the tree stump stood an oak, so big it took a rabbit many hops to go round its trunk. Wisher waited until her parr was looking up at the sky for Burdock, then made a dash for the tree. When she was quite sure he wasn't looking, she slipped away unnoticed.

Wisher remembered first meeting
Parsley by a molehill and hoped she
could find the same one again. But
when she looked around she saw lots of
molehills dotted about the meadow. They
all looked alike. Oh dear, she thought.
How am I ever going to find Parsley?

Wisher set off towards a group of
molehills, clustered near a gate in the
field. As she hopped along by a fence,
she began to think more about Blinker's
news. Everyone seemed upset about the
dogs. But what had happened to the
piglet? Any animal that was being chased,
she decided, was an animal in trouble.
She tried to imagine how *she* would feel
being chased by Burdock, or a fox, or the
dreaded Red Dragon.

Arriving at the gate, Wisher slipped underneath and came nose to nose with a very strange animal indeed. It was brown and white and had long legs, and had a big, round nose. The animal sniffed, then gave Wisher a lick with its rough, pink tongue.

Wisher laughed.

"Hey," she said, tumbling over backwards. "That tickles!"

"*Moo!*" said the long-legged creature, swishing its tail.

The animal seemed huge to Wisher, but somehow she didn't feel afraid.

"Are you a piglet?" she asked.

"Do I look like a piglet?" the animal said. "No, I am not!" It scampered away, leaving Wisher no wiser than before.

Wisher set off again to look for Parsley. Near the river, she hopped into a patch of long grass where bluebells, tall cow parsley and golden buttercups grew. Suddenly she felt her ears tingle – the way they had when she'd been with Bramble, Bracken, Berry and Fern on their first day out of the warren. And again she heard the mysterious voice, whispering a warning:

I whisper a song like the wind in your ear.
Wisher, beware. Wisher, take care!

"Oh," said Wisher. "I wonder what's the matter this time?"

She swallowed hard and looked nervously about. She was on her own and felt afraid, wondering what might happen. A split second later, she saw the shadow of hovering, outstretched wings only a few hops away. Wisher stopped in her tracks. She knew the shape of those enormous wings and who they belonged to. Before Wisher could take another breath, down from the sky swooped Burdock!

The buzzard dived towards a crouching, quivering field mouse. Wisher shut her eyes tight. She couldn't be certain, but she *thought* the mouse had escaped just in time.

When she
dared look
again, Burdock was
flying up into a tree to
perch. Oh no! she thought.
I'm in big trouble. He's sure to see
me! Her heart was beating so hard, she
was sure the buzzard would hear it. I
should have listened to Parr and Marr. I
wish I was at home. Run, run, back to the
burrow, was all she could think.

Frantically she looked about for the
oak, Parr's favourite tree stump, *anything*
near her warren. But there was nothing.
Which way *is* home? she thought in a
panic.

Wisher risked another glance at
Burdock. He had his head tucked under
one wing and was preening his feathers.
Wisher saw her chance to escape.

Plucking up all her
courage, she made a
dash for the nearest
cover – a fallen tree
across the river.

The sudden
movement alerted Burdock at once. With his
powerful eyesight, he easily spotted Wisher's
white fur and bobbing tail as she raced across
the ground.

"Rabbit!" exclaimed Burdock, swooping to
snatch her.

Burdock was quick, but not quick enough.
He was so close Wisher could hear the *swish!*
of his wings. She darted this way. That
way. Faster and faster until, with a leap, she
landed on the tree trunk and hid among the
branches, panting. Then, to Wisher's relief,

Burdock lost sight of her and she watched him fly away.

After a while, Wisher thought it might be safe to move. She hopped across the trunk to the other side of the river, then ran in what she hoped was the right direction for her warren. She kept going, and didn't stop until she came to a stone bridge.

"I've never seen *this* bridge before," she said to herself. "Oh, I'm lost! I'll never find my way home."

The ground here was marshy, not at all like the short, dry turf near the warren. Mud oozed between Wisher's paws, which she hated.

"Ugh!" she said, shaking her hind foot. "I don't like it here. I'll climb the bank. It'll be dry up there. Perhaps I'll see my home from the top."

Wisher scuttled up the bank hopefully and, to her surprise, came face to face with another strange creature. This animal was smaller than the one she'd met earlier. This one had big black splotches all over his plump little body, a pink snout and a tightly curled tail.

"Are *you* a piglet?" Wisher asked.

"Yes I am!" the animal replied.

Pig on the Line
6

Wisher and Foster stared at each other. Foster was the first to speak. He had been sitting on the bank for some time feeling sorry for himself, so he was pleased to see somebody to talk to.

"Hello," he said, getting up and coming towards her. "I'm Foster. Who are you?"

"I'm Wisher," said Wisher, taking a few steps backwards. After her near escape from Burdock, she wasn't taking any chances. This piglet could be dangerous! Then she saw Foster's eyes were red, as though he'd been crying. He didn't *look* very threatening.

"Are you the *runaway* piglet?" she asked.

"Yes," said Foster. He quickly told Wisher the whole story. "And now I'm lost and *very* hungry," he finished.

At this, Wisher looked alarmed.

"Do piglets eat rabbits?" she asked nervously.

"Ugh! Disgusting! No thanks!" said Foster. He pictured Fred Fairweather bringing his breakfast earlier that morning. He could almost smell the milky swill! Foster told Wisher about the delicious food the farmer fed him at the Farm Park. "I wish I was back there now. But I don't know which way to go. And that nasty dog might still be out there."

Wisher knew exactly how Foster felt. She was lost and homesick too. She was just wondering how she could help the piglet and find her own way home, when she felt a tingling in her ears and heard a voice whispering:

I whisper a song like the wind in your ear. Wisher, beware. Wisher, take care!

Suddenly Wisher saw where they were sitting. They were right in the middle of the Red Dragon's tracks! She had been so busy listening to Foster, she hadn't noticed them. The tracks started to shake, shuddering under the weight of something heavy and fast. To Wisher's horror, she heard a shrieking sound and saw something big – scarily big – rounding a corner of the track, clattering and rattling along, belching clouds of smoke and charging straight towards where she and Foster were sitting.

It was the Red Dragon!

Wisher and Foster were fixed to the spot with fear. The Red Dragon deafened them with its piercing whistles, shrieking again and again for them to get out of its way. Next she heard an awful screeching sound as the Red Dragon came to a halt.

Wisher faced the terrifying monster, her heart thudding in her chest. The massive red beast towered above them, blasting out its hot, steamy breath. From somewhere high above their heads they heard a shout:

"Pig on the line!"

Wisher and Foster looked up to see many smiling people-folk gazing down at them. Wisher remembered seeing humans, as Parsley had called them, the first time he had shown her where the Red Dragon lived. And here they were again, riding on the Red Dragon, just the way Parsley had described. Wisher thought it was an odd thing to do, but the people-folk looked very happy, and she wasn't scared.

Foster, however, who was recovering from the shock of almost being run over by the train, wasn't taking any chances.

"I've been chased by a dog and nearly flattened," said Foster. "I've had enough for one day. I'm off!"

"No, wait," said Wisher. She had spotted one of the people-folk walking towards them, holding an apple. "Look, Foster. I think she wants to help you."

Foster looked longingly at the apple. His tummy was rumbling more noisily than ever and felt as hollow as an empty barrel. He was so hungry he could have faced a hundred steam trains for just one bite.

"Go on," whispered Wisher. "I've got a good feeling about this. She looks very friendly. I'm sure she'll take care of you."

Foster thought of the visitors who came every day to Fairweather's Farm

Park, riding on the steam train. *They* were friendly. And, although he'd only just met Wisher, somehow he felt he could trust her.

"You're right," said Foster, cheering up. "Thank you, Wisher!"

A few minutes later, he allowed himself to be carried on to the train.

As Wisher watched him leave, she saw Foster happily munching the apple, juice dribbling down his chin.

Back at Fairweather's Farm Park, Agatha Old Spot was anxiously awaiting news of Foster. It had been nearly two hours since her piglet had been chased from the farmyard by the dog, Toby, and she was worried sick. She couldn't eat a thing. Still, she was pleased to see that Foster's sudden disappearance hadn't affected the appetite of his brothers and sisters – Fred Fairweather had brought a fresh bucket of breakfast, and the six little Gloucester Old Spots had heartily tucked in.

Agatha had also seen Toby being grabbed by his mistress and told off for causing so much trouble. Toby was now attached to a lead, although that didn't stop him remarking to Mrs Woolly as he passed by: "Don't know what all the fuss was about. I was only having fun!"

As Agatha waited, she heard the sound of the train whistle as it approached the Farm Park. Soon there would be more visitors arriving, but she was in no mood for people-folk today. Sadly she sat in a corner of her sty, wondering if she would *ever* see Foster again. Then she saw Fred Fairweather striding across the yard.

He was carrying something wrapped in a blanket, and Agatha caught a glimpse of two pink ears poking out of the top.

Agatha heaved herself up and ran across the sty to the door. Excitedly she peered at the bundle in Fred's arms. Could it be? Dare she hope? Then she was sure.

"I'd know those ears anywhere," said Agatha as Fred came in. "Foster!" she cried. "You're back!"

Later, after Foster had eaten an enormous meal, he told his family about his adventure. He finished his story:

". . . and then I met a rabbit called

Wisher. I think she was lost too. But she helped me. I like Wisher. I hope she finds her way home."

"So do I," said Agatha. "Wisher sounds like a very special little rabbit."

And that evening the Gloucester Old Spots curled up together happily and went to sleep.

Foster's story was the talk of the Farm Park. Mrs Woolly told the geese next door . . . then Gilbert the goose hurried off to tell Daisy Duck. Soon, the story of Wisher and the runaway piglet was making its way along the riverbank . . .

A Lucky Escape
7

Wisher waited until the Red Dragon was out of sight before she set off again. She was glad she'd met the piglet – quite by chance, as it happened. And she'd been relieved to hear there had only been *one* dog on the loose after all.

"Although," she said as she scampered down a steep bank, "even one dog is bad enough! I'd still like to warn Parsley. If only I knew where he was."

Wisher hopped along, hoping she

was going the right way for home. She imagined Foster safely back with his mother, and felt homesick for her warren. She'd give anything to be there now with Marr and Parr, Bramble, Bracken, Berry and Fern. She wondered what they were doing. Perhaps they were all looking for her. Wisher knew she'd been away too long and her parents would be worried. If only she knew how to get home.

Suddenly, Wisher remembered being chased by Burdock. That had been very frightening. And supposing she was spotted by the horrid dog? Foster had managed to outrun it, but could she? She looked nervously around, then told herself not to be so silly. After all, hadn't she just faced the Red Dragon?

"Nothing could be worse than that," she said out loud.

"Worse than what?" said a voice from behind.

Wisher spun round, dreading what she might find. The dog? Burdock? Or, maybe a hungry fox . . .

"Parsley!" she cried. "Oh, I'm so pleased to see you. I've been looking for you everywhere."

The two friends sat and talked. Wisher had so much to tell Parsley, but he seemed to know quite a lot already.

"Everyone's talking about you," said Parsley.

"Apparently you stopped the Red
Dragon in his tracks by holding up your
paw!"

Wisher's eyes opened wide in disbelief.

"I didn't . . ." she began.

Parsley laughed.

"Guessed as much," he said. "But
you know how these stories get about.
Anyway, one thing's true. I've heard your
parents are frantic with worry. You must
go home."

"I don't know the way!" wailed Wisher.
"I'm completely lost."

"Tunnels," said Parsley. "Didn't I say
the other day? Tunnels are a great way
to get about. Allow me to show you my
new tunnel, Wisher. It's your quickest way
home. Come on!"

Wisher followed Parsley down
a hole into his tunnel. It was very
narrow in places, like before, but in
no time at all it seemed to Wisher
that they were travelling up a slope
and out into the fresh air.

Wisher knew where they were
straightaway. Parsley's new tunnel
had brought them out at the oak, just
a few hops from her home. And there
was Parr on his tree stump and Marr
by the burrow, looking out for her.

"Thank you, Parsley!" said Wisher.
"See you again very soon."

"Yes," said Parsley. "Up the
Burrowers! Goodbye!" And he
disappeared underground.

"Wisher!" cried Barley and Mellow, running to meet her. "Oh, Wisher, where have you been? We've been SO worried."

Wisher could hardly breathe her parents were hugging her so tightly. They were both talking at once, so fast she only heard snatches of what they were saying.

"They said you were nearly eaten by the Dragon . . . chased by the piglet too . . . at least *ten* wild dogs on your tail . . . you had a lucky escape . . . never go wandering off on your own again!"

Wisher couldn't get a word in to explain what had really happened. Perhaps one day she would tell them, but not now.

That night, as Mellow tucked Wisher into bed, she said:

"You've had quite an adventure."

Wisher smiled dreamily back at her mother.

Yes, she thought. And I've a feeling there'll be many more to come!

Author's Note

The view from my cottage window overlooking the Kensey Valley, North Cornwall, and the Launceston Steam Railway were my inspiration for writing *The Railway Rabbits*. The route of the railway, which runs along this unspoilt river valley, links the once ancient capital of Cornwall with New Mills Farm Park and provided me with the perfect setting for my adventurous rabbits.

I began my research in January 2010, by visiting the owners of the railway, Kay and Nigel Bowman. Sitting in the Station Café they told me about their railway and some of the weird and wonderful things they'd seen, whilst driving the trains.

Yes, Kay is a train driver too! And I rode on the footplate of a bright, red locomotive called Covertcoat, which became my inspiration for the Red Dragon. The idea for the first book, *Wisher and the Runaway Piglet*, was based on a real pig that had wandered on to the line. I'm not sure if that pig was carried home on the train, but it makes a good story!

The stories are told mostly from the rabbit's point of view and, from this perspective, these are big adventures for little rabbits. I've tried to convey a sense of reality about the dangers rabbits face living in the wild – the Longears' number one enemy is Burdock the buzzard. I often see one of these magnificent birds circling overhead, or sitting on a telegraph pole in our meadow.

I hope you enjoy reading all the books in this series as much as I've enjoyed writing them. My thanks to my family and the many people who have helped me along the way. I'm particularly grateful to Kay and Nigel Bowman at Launceston Steam Railway; to Richard and Sandra Ball at New Mills Farm Park; my agent, Rosemary Sandberg and everyone at Orion Children's Books, with special thanks to my publisher, Fiona Kennedy; editor Jenny Glencross; designers Loulou Clark and Abi Hartshorne, and to Anna Currey for her wonderful illustrations.

Georgie Adams
Cornwall, 2014

www.georgieadams.com
www.orionbooks.co.uk

Look out for . . .

Bramble and the Easter Egg

*Join the Railway Rabbits: Barley, Mellow,
Bramble, Bracken, Berry, Fern and Wisher
Longears in their adventures.*

Bramble is fed up – he never gets to do anything
exciting. Then he hears a story about golden
eggs and sets off to find one for himself.

978 1 4440 1216 3
£4.99

the orion star

CALLING ALL GROWN-UPS!
Sign up for **the orion star** newsletter to
hear about your favourite authors and exclusive
competitions, plus details of how children
can join our 'Story Stars' review panel.

Sign up at:

www.orionbooks.co.uk/orionstar

Follow us 🐦 @the_orionstar
Find us 📘 facebook.com/TheOrionStar